MAX
THE BOY WHO MADE A MILLION

Collins
R E D
STORYBOOK

MAX
THE BOY WHO MADE A MILLION

GYLES BRANDRETH

Illustrated by Mark Edwards

CollinsChildren'sBooks

An imprint of HarperCollins*Publishers*

First published in Great Britain by
CollinsChildren'sBooks 1996

3 5 7 9 8 6 4

CollinsChildren'sBooks is a division of HarperCollins*Publishers* Ltd,
77-85 Fulham Palace Road, Hammersmith, London W6 8JB.

The HarperCollins website address is
www.**fire**and**water**.com

Text copyright © Gyles Brandreth 1996
Illustrations copyright © Mark Edwards 1996

Gyles Brandreth and Mark Edwards assert their rights to be identified
respectively as the author and illustrator of this work.

Printed and bound in Great Britain
by Caledonian International Book Manufacturing Ltd, Glasgow G64

ISBN HB 0 00 185665 0
ISBN PB 0 00 675227 6

CONTENTS

Chapter One
'RICH IS POOR'

I was born on Christmas Eve in the year 1888. I don't remember it, of course. I know that the moon was full that night, and that the snow fell steadily, because my father told me so. I don't remember my mother because she died a few minutes after I was born. I know she was beautiful because, as I write this, I am looking at my father's favourite photograph of her. Pasted on the back of the photograph is a cutting from the *New York Times*:

DEATH OF MRS TOBIAS RICH, CELEBRATED
ACTRESS AND NOTED BEAUTY

My mother was very beautiful and my father was very handsome. He was also very kind. And very, very rich. At least, he was very rich until the day he lost a million dollars. That's the day I want to tell you about. It's the day my story begins. It's an amazing story, fantastic even, but, believe me, every word of it is true. Fantastic things do happen. They happened to me.

`*

Miss Taylor was my governess. She was lovely and I loved her very much. That day she had dressed me in my best brown velvet suit and I remember she brushed my hair so hard that my head hurt. At the end of my lessons, she took me by the hand and said to me very softly, 'Today, Max, your father has something important to tell you. He wants to see you in the drawing room.'

The drawing room was the largest room you ever saw. I only went into it twice in my life. It had double doors that seemed to open by magic and there were huge mirrors framed in gold on every wall. My father was standing with his back to the fireplace and, as I

'I'VE GOT SOME BAD NEWS FOR YOU, MAX.'

came into the room and looked around me in amazement, he clapped his hands and said, 'Max, you'll soon be eight years of age. You'll soon be quite grown up. We need to talk. But first, we're going to toast some muffins!'

The fire was so hot it burned my cheeks and made my eyes smart. My father crouched down by my side. He steadied my hand as I held out the toasting fork towards the leaping flames. The muffins smelt good. When each one had turned a golden brown my father prised it quickly from the end of the fork and dropped it on to a silver dish. Miss Taylor spread the muffins with cold, hard butter that was bright yellow and melted at once.

My father poured drinking chocolate, steaming hot, from a large silver jug into three small green and gold cups and said, 'Boy, toasting muffins by your own fireside is the closest you will get to true happiness in this world. Isn't that right, Miss Taylor?'

Miss Taylor looked up at my father and smiled. I loved that smile of hers. It made her eyes shine. Miss Taylor was very special. She taught me how to read and how to write and how to say my prayers. She taught me to chew every mouthful of food fifteen times before swallowing. She also taught me a wonderful card trick and, when we went out for our daily walk in Central Park, if she was sure no one was looking, she showed me how to turn cartwheels. She was my best friend.

When we had finished eating all the muffins, my father stood up and turned towards the fireplace and put his hands on the big marble mantelpiece. He looked at me in the mirror and smiled. 'I've got some bad news for you, Max,' he said. 'You're going to have to be brave, boy, brave and strong.'

'What is it?' I said. 'What's wrong?'

'Your father has lost all his money,' a different voice answered. It was a voice I knew well. I looked up at the mirror and saw the reflection of Dr Webster who was standing by the door.

My father laughed sadly. 'Yes,' he said, 'Rich is poor!'

Dr Webster was my father's business partner and his oldest friend. I hated him. He was fat and ugly.

His hands were always sticky and he smelt of tobacco.

'It's a bad business, Maximilian,' he said, sucking on a small cigar and shaking his head. 'Your father's lost a million.'

My father put his hand on my shoulder, gently. 'This big old house of ours is going to be sold, son. You're going to have to live somewhere new.'

'I don't mind where we live,' I said, 'so long as we're together.'

'That's just it, Max...' My father turned away.

'In future, Maximilian,' growled Dr Webster, 'you're going to live in a children's home.'

'No!' I shouted at Dr Webster. 'I want to live with Dad. And with Miss Taylor.'

'You're going to live in a children's home, Maximilian, and I'm taking you there tomorrow.'

'No! No!'

'Your father's going away, Max.' Miss Taylor had tears in her eyes.

Dr Webster sneered, 'Your father's going to prison, Maximilian.'

'No! No! No!' With my eyes stinging and my heart pounding, I pushed past Dr Webster and ran towards the door. Miss Taylor tried to catch me, but my father turned and stopped her.

'Don't,' he said gently. 'Let him go. Leave him be.'

I ran out of the drawing room and up the great staircase. When I reached my room I locked the door and threw myself on to my four-poster bed. 'You're going to have to be brave, boy, brave and strong,' my father had said.

That night I made my plan.

Chapter Two
ESCAPE

It was a simple enough plan. If my father needed a million dollars to stay out of jail I'd find a million dollars! I decided, there and then, to run away and make my fortune.

I hated Dr Webster. I hated his horrible tobacco smell. I hated his hot, horrible, sticky hands. I knew I had to escape before he could take me to his horrible children's home. I knew I couldn't risk saying goodbye to my father or Miss Taylor. I knew I had to get away without anybody knowing.

As soon as the house was still and I was certain no one was about, I tucked my lucky silver dime into my pocket – and slipped silently out of my room. On tiptoe, carefully avoiding the floor-boards that creaked, I crept along the corridor, past my father's room, past Miss Taylor's room, down the back stairs to the kitchen. I secured my supplies – bread, cheese, lemonade.

There was a door off the kitchen leading to a front area with a narrow flight of steps going up to 55th Street. (Our house was on the corner of 55th Street and Fifth Avenue.) The door was locked and bolted and the key was not hanging where I expected it to be. I made my way back up from the kitchen to the hallway, but the front door was locked and bolted too. I would have to escape through a window.

I pushed open the big double doors leading to the drawing room. The fire had gone out and the room was in darkness. I ran over to the large window that looked straight out on to Fifth Avenue. The street was deserted.

Suddenly, I heard footsteps in the hall. And voices.

Quickly, I hid behind the long velvet drapes as my father, holding an oil lamp, and Dr Webster, smoking one of his evil-smelling cigars, came into the room. For what seemed like an hour I stood there like a statue while they talked and talked.

I did not understand a lot of what I heard, but I understood enough to know that my father and Dr Webster had been raising money to buy some land and build a theatre – 'Rich's Playhouse,' my father called it, 'the most beautiful, the biggest and the best theatre in the world'.

The money had come from friends, from other business people, from banks, but somehow all of it, every cent, had disappeared. Because it was my father who had signed all the papers, he was going to be arrested in the morning and put on trial for fraud.

'I am an innocent man, Webster,' said my father. 'And you know it.'

'You signed all the documents,' said Dr Webster, lighting another cigar.

'You made me do it.'

'Can you prove that?'

'No, I can't prove anything. It's just your word against mine.'

'Exactly.' Dr Webster laughed and walked towards the door. 'You'll say I'm guilty and I'll say you're guilty and the jury will believe me because you signed the papers and I didn't. Unless I confess, and I don't plan to do that, prison is where you're going and prison is where you'll stay. Good night, Rich. And goodbye.'

As they left the drawing room, I whispered to myself, 'Be brave, Dad, be brave and strong. I'll find your million dollars. I'll make Dr Webster confess. I'll do it. You wait and see.'

*

Early the next morning the police came and arrested Dad. As soon as he had been taken away, Dr Webster and Miss Taylor started searching for me. They searched high and low. They looked everywhere, including, of course, the drawing room.

Dr Webster pulled back the drapes by the big window that looked out on to Fifth Avenue. I wasn't there.

'What's this?' he growled. 'Bread and cheese? Was he hiding here last night?'

'What do you mean?' asked Miss Taylor.

'Nothing,' he muttered. 'He's not here. At least that's clear. The little pest has run away.'

'He'll come back.'

'There'll be nothing to come back to,' Dr Webster snarled. 'The boy can stay on the run till the police catch up with him. He's no better than his father.'

I heard Miss Taylor sobbing.

'There's no point in crying, woman. They've gone. It's all over. You'd better pack your bags and get going too. Goodbye.'

Miss Taylor didn't answer. I heard her climbing the stairs and, a little later, I heard her letting herself out of the front door. I wondered if I would ever see her again.

Where had I been hiding? Can you guess? Yes, I had climbed up inside the chimney in the drawing room. There were holes in the chimney wall, like little steps, so that the sweeps could climb up to clear away the soot. About five feet up there was a small ledge, it was warm and snug, and that's where I perched all day and all night and all through a second day until all the noisy activity in the house had stopped and I was certain that the house was deserted. I had nothing to eat because, stupidly, I had dropped the bread and cheese behind the drapes. All I had in the world was a bottle of lemonade and my lucky silver dime.

When, at last, it was safe to clamber down into the drawing room, I found it quite empty – the sofas, the chairs, the tables, the ornaments, the rugs, even the drapes, had all gone. I heard the church clock of St Bartholomew's strike midnight as I broke a pane of glass in the drawing room window and, slowly and carefully, climbed through. 'Max,' I said to myself, 'this is going to be some adventure!'

It was.

*

Standing in the street outside our house, hungry and all alone, I had no idea where to go or even which way to turn. I had no money except for the lucky silver dime that Miss Taylor had given me for my birthday. I tossed it. 'Heads I go left, tails I go right.'

It was heads. I turned to the left and began walking up the empty street. The night was cold and still, and very quiet. I reached the corner. Which way now? I tossed my lucky dime. Heads again. I turned down Sixth Avenue. There was a horse and carriage coming towards me. I pulled into a doorway until it had passed. 'You're going to have to be brave, boy, brave and strong.' That was what my father had said.

I stepped out of the doorway and started running down the street. As I got nearer the next corner I saw the figure of a man standing under a lamppost. It was a policeman. I stopped. He turned. I held my breath. He began to walk towards me. Had he seen me? I couldn't be sure. I took my bottle of lemonade and flung it as hard and high into the air as I could. It crashed at the foot of the lamppost and smashed into a dozen pieces. The policeman spun round to see what had happened. I ran on.

I ran and I ran and I ran. My heart was pounding so fast and so loud I couldn't tell if the policeman was running after me. I came to another corner.

I KEPT RUNNING UNTIL I COULD RUN NO MORE.

There was no time to toss my lucky dime. I turned into the side street. It was much darker and narrower. I kept running until I could run no more. I had reached a dead end. At the far end of the street I could just hear the policeman's footsteps. Ahead of me all I could see was a huge brick wall with a metal ladder going straight up the side of it. As the policeman's footsteps got louder I jumped on to the bottom rung of the ladder and began to climb. Higher and higher I went. I began to count the rungs. Twenty, thirty, forty... seventy, eighty, eighty-four, eighty-five – and then, over a stone ledge, and I was on the roof. I stopped. Above me was the clear night sky. Below me, a long way below, the dark streets of New York. I couldn't hear the policeman's footsteps now.

The roof was wide and flat, and right in the middle of it was a skylight, a kind of large square window let into the roof itself. With the cold wind blowing round me, I scrambled towards it. Luckily, it was open and the gap was wide enough for me to squeeze through. Hanging down inside was another ladder, a wooden one with just eight rungs. Slowly, carefully, I climbed down it and jumped off.

I seemed to have landed in a long, curving corridor. There were doors on either side and the one just ahead of me was open. There was flickering candlelight dancing on the wall. As I tried to tiptoe past, very gently the door swung completely open.

Lying on a long sofa in the middle of the room was a tall, thin man dressed in elegant evening clothes, with a shiny top hat pushed over his eyes.

'Excuse me,' I stammered, not knowing what to say. 'Are you some sort of ghost?'

'Far from it,' said the tall, thin gentleman, lifting his hat and nodding his head in a kind of greeting. 'I'm sorry you don't recognise me, young man. I am The Great Zapristi!'

Chapter Three
THE GREAT ZAPRISTI

'The great who?' I asked.

'The Great Zapristi!' he roared, getting to his feet and grabbing a silver-topped cane off the dressing table. For a second I thought he was going to bring the cane crashing down on to my head. Instead he jabbed it towards a large poster hanging on the wall. 'Can't you read, boy?'

'Not very well, sir.'

'It says, "The Great Zapristi – Man of a Million Secrets – Master of Illusion – Famous the World

Over!"'

'Are you some kind of magician then?' I asked.

'Some kind of magician!' he exploded again. 'I am Zapristi!' He lifted the silver-topped cane and as he banged it down on to the dressing table it turned instantly into a spectacular bouquet of flowers.

'Wow!' I gasped. 'That's great.'

'That's Zapristi!' said the mysterious gentleman, and he gave a little bow. 'And who are you, may I ask?'

'I'm Rich,' I said.

'That's good,' he chuckled and made a smacking noise with his lips.

'No, that's my name. I'm Maximilian Rich. My friends call me Max.'

'I shall call you "Ali, the Boy Wonder, Son of a Sultan and Rising Star of the East!"'

'Why?'

'Because The Great Zapristi can't have an assistant called Max, that's why.'

'But who says I'm going to be your assistant?'

'Don't you want to be my assistant?' he said,

throwing the bouquet of flowers on to the sofa. 'Don't you want to make your fortune and travel the world?'

'Well, sir, you see, I—' I didn't know what to say.

'Of course you do,' thundered Zapristi, bending over and pulling a wicker basket out from under the dressing table. 'I take it you've run away from home?'

'Yes,' I stammered, 'but—'

'You've got no food, no money, no place to go, no clothes apart from the ones you're standing in?' He opened the basket and produced a bright orange turban from it.

'How do you know all this?'

'The Great Zapristi knows everything!' he said, with another chuckle, as he pulled the turban over my ears. 'A million dollars has gone missing. Your father has been arrested. Until the money is recovered he's going to be locked up in jail!'

'Are you a mind reader as well?' I gasped.

'I read minds, of course I do,' he said, with a shrug. 'I also read the evening newspaper and I'm afraid your dad's on the front page.'

'He's done nothing wrong, I know it,' I protested.

'I believe you,' said Zapristi with a smile. 'The trouble seems to be the missing million...'

'My father is innocent!' I shouted.

'If you say so,' chuckled Zapristi.

'I don't just say so,' I cried, 'I know so! Dr Webster stole the money and made it look as if it was my father. He's the one who should be in jail. I'm going to free my father! I'm going to make a million! Whatever it takes, I'm going to do it!'

'That's the spirit!' smiled Zapristi, pulling a shiny green cape out of the basket and tying it around my shoulders. 'I can't promise you as much as a million, but I can offer you food, lodging and a dollar a week to start with. What do you say?'

I didn't say anything.

'"Thank you, Zapristi," is what you ought to say,' he went on, pinning a bright silver star to the front of the turban. 'How old are you, boy?'

'I'm eight, sir. Well almost.'

'Is that all?' he burst out. 'My last assistant was three times your age and she only got a dollar a week!'

'I SHALL CALL YOU ALI, THE BOY WONDER!'

'Isn't she with you any more?' I asked.

'No,' he said, with a heavy sigh. 'She ran off to join the circus.'

'Won't she come back?'

He shook his head. 'I'm afraid not,' he said. 'She was eaten by a lion. It was a sad end to a promising career. I had high hopes for her – just as I have for you, my boy.'

He put his hands on my shoulders and swivelled me round so that I could see myself in the mirror. 'The costume suits you,' he said with satisfaction. 'What do you say, young man? Do we have a deal?'

I couldn't think what to say, so I said, 'Yes'.

'Excellent!' cried Zapristi and, as he clapped his hands, the air was filled with a bright cloud of sparkling gold dust.

Chapter Four
THE BOY WONDER

That night I slept curled up at the bottom of Zapristi's costume basket. The next morning I began my new life as 'Ali, the Boy Wonder, Son of a Sultan and Rising Star of the East'.

The building I had climbed into turned out to be the Adelphi Theatre, a music hall off 54th Street, where, twice nightly and three times on Saturday, we presented a spectacular entertainment called 'The New York All Stars'. The performers included singers and dancers, comedians and acrobats, a

Mexican who played the xylophone wearing a blindfold, two Bulgarian brothers who rode unicycles, and an Italian lady opera singer who sang duets with an African parrot – as well, of course, as me and The Great Zapristi.

Even though it said on the poster that Zapristi was 'famous the world over' we still only had eight minutes on stage and our dressing room was the smallest in the building and the one nearest the roof.

The person who seemed to be in charge of the show was a little man with a wizened face like a monkey. He had a small beard, silver and ginger, and a Scottish accent that was so strong I could hardly understand him. Everyone called him 'Big Mac' or 'Boss'.

'Boss,' said Zapristi, introducing me on that first morning, 'may I present my new assistant, Ali, the Boy Wonder.'

Big Mac raised a suspicious eyebrow. 'He dunno look all that wonderful to me,' he snorted. 'He's no more than a shrimp. What do you plan to do with the wee laddie?'

'Throw daggers at him,' said Zapristi, smacking his lips, 'poke swords through him, cut him in half – and then make him disappear!'

Big Mac raised both his eyebrows now. 'Och aye?' he said. 'And can the wee laddie do anything for himself?'

'I can do the card trick Miss Taylor taught me,' I said. 'And I can do this—' And I began to cartwheel across the stage.

'I like it!' said Big Mac, with a grunt of approval.

I am happy to say the audience liked it too. That night, dressed as an Indian prince, I cartwheeled on to the stage of the Adelphi Theatre for the very first time and everybody cheered. They cheered even more loudly when The Great Zapristi made me stand at the side of the stage and threw nine daggers at me. Four landed either side of my arms. Four landed either side of my legs. With the last dagger, Zapristi pierced an apple that he had balanced on top of my head.

'And now, ladies and gentlemen,' he announced, swirling his black cape around him, 'I will ask Ali, the

Boy Wonder, to step into my magic cabinet.'

In the centre of the stage was a large, wooden box, square like a packing case. I stepped inside and crouched down so that Zapristi could close the box. Once the lid was down, I quickly lifted a wide wooden slat out of the floor of the box and squeezed myself into its false bottom.

'Are you in there, Ali?' called Zapristi.

'Yes, sir,' I shouted from inside the false bottom.

'Good!' he exclaimed, and he began to push five swords through the box, one through the centre of each side, one from top to bottom. The audience gasped. Zapristi pulled out the five swords.

'Are you in there, Ali?' he called a second time.

'No, sir,' I shouted back.

'Good!' he roared, opening the lid of the box and pulling it forward to show the audience the inside of the empty cabinet. As he slammed shut the lid of the box, the audience applauded and, unnoticed, I slipped out of the bottom of the cabinet, and hid behind Zapristi.

'Where's the little rascal gone?' asked the great

HE BEGAN TO PUSH FIVE SWORDS THROUGH THE BOX.

illusionist, and, as he swirled his cape in the air again, I cartwheeled out from behind him and the audience cheered.

I liked my new life with The Great Zapristi. When we were performing on stage, when he was showing me new tricks in his dressing room, when, on Sundays, we went out to Coney Island to see the new Ferris Wheel or ride on the roller-coaster, I thought I was the happiest and luckiest boy in the world. But, at night, curled up at the bottom of Zapristi's costume basket, I remembered that my dad was locked up in prison and I felt cold and sad and frightened and lonely. I wanted to see Miss Taylor. I wanted to cry. 'You're going to have to be brave, boy, brave and strong.'

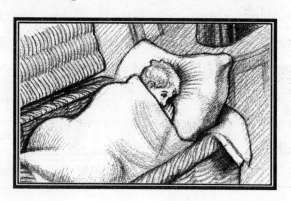

One Saturday night, when I had been with The Great Zapristi for about eight weeks, at the end of the performance Big Mac called everybody on to the stage. 'Grim tidings, ladies and gentlemen...' he began.

I whispered to Zapristi, 'What does he mean?'

'He means it's all over,' sighed Zapristi. 'The show's off. We've had a good run for our money, but the audiences are getting smaller so it's time to call it a day. That's showbusiness!'

'What's going to happen to us?'

'I shall leave the country,' said Zapristi with a smile.

'Where will you go?'

'To England – and I'm taking you with me.'

'But what about my father? What about the money?' I held up the cardboard shoebox containing the eight dollars I had saved so far.

'We're going to London, Max. Haven't you heard the streets of London are paved with gold?'

'Really?'

'Yes, really. You can make your fortune there.'

'I can't come,' I said.

'You must come,' snorted Zapristi. 'Besides, if you don't, who will I have to saw in half?'

'When do you plan to go?' I asked.

'Right now,' he said, and he smacked his lips.

Chapter Five
STOWAWAYS

Big Mac was still on stage talking to the other performers when we left the Adelphi Theatre for the last time. Zapristi must have known what was going to happen because he had already packed all his costumes and props into the wicker basket and strapped the basket and both his magic cabinets to a large barrow that was waiting for us by the stage door.

As we pushed the barrow slowly down the narrow side street and reached the corner, I turned to have one final look at the theatre that had been my unusual home for the past two months.

'Don't look back,' said Zapristi sternly. 'Never look back. Only look ahead. Think, an hour from now we could be starting the greatest adventure of our lives!'

In fact, an hour later we were still tramping slowly through the streets of New York. It took us until two in the morning to reach the shore of the Hudson River.

'Here we are!' said Zapristi triumphantly. 'The port of New York, the busiest harbour in the world! Every day ships sail from here to the four corners of the earth.'

Standing on the dockside, looking to the left or right, as far as the eye could see, there were ships – ships of every description and every size, tug boats, yachts, paddle steamers, dinghies, ferries, ocean-going liners, the smaller ones moving up and down gently in the swell of the water, the larger ones lying massive and still, firmly moored to the quayside with great ropes tied to iron bollards.

'It's very quiet,' I said.

'It's the middle of the night,' said Zapristi. 'They're all tucked up in their cabins. Have you ever slept in a hammock, my boy?'

'No, but I'd like to,' I said, thinking that it would probably be a lot more comfortable than sleeping in the bottom of a wicker basket.

'This looks like the one for us,' said Zapristi, suddenly putting down the barrow. 'Where's your lucky dime?'

'What do you mean?'

'Heads, this is our boat; tails, it isn't.'

I tossed the lucky dime. It was heads. 'But are you sure this is sailing to England?' I asked. 'Don't we have to have tickets and passports and things?'

'Not if we're stowaways,' said Zapristi, smacking his lips. 'Come on!'

There was a long narrow gangplank leading up from the quayside to the deck of the ship. 'We'll come back for the luggage,' whispered Zapristi. 'Be as quiet as a mouse.' On tiptoes he led the way up the gangplank. At the top, lying back in a deck chair, fast asleep and snoring loudly, was a sailor. 'He must be

'HE MUST BE ON GUARD DUTY...'

on guard duty,' chuckled Zapristi.

We crept past the sleeping sailor and moved quickly across the deck towards three rowing boats that were lined up on the far side. Each was covered with a tarpaulin sheet. 'Perfect!' hissed Zapristi gleefully. 'We'll hide in here.'

We crept back across the deck, tiptoed down the gangplank, and carefully lifted the wicker basket and the magic cabinets off the barrow.

'We'll carry them up one at a time,' whispered Zapristi. 'You take that end.' We struggled up the narrow gangplank three times and each time we passed the sleeping sailor his snoring seemed to get louder.

'What do we do if he wakes up?' I asked.

'Tell him he's having a nightmare!' chortled Zapristi.

To my amazement, and relief, the sailor didn't wake up. Carefully we untied the knots that fixed the tarpaulin to the lifeboats and managed to fit the basket and both the cabinets into one of them.

'So far so good,' whispered Zapristi.

'No it isn't!' I exclaimed. 'Where's my shoebox? Where's the money?'

'Shsh!' hissed Zapristi. 'Not so loud! It's probably still on the barrow.'

Quickly, I ran back past the snoring sailor and down the gangplank. The barrow was still there and my cardboard box was on it, but there was something strange, something odd about the barrow. It seemed to have been moved and there was a horrible smell of cigar smoke in the air.

I grabbed my box and ran back up the gangplank as fast as I could. I found Zapristi and together we counted out the money. Eight dollars. It was all still there.

'You're starting to imagine things, my boy,' said Zapristi. 'What you need is a long sea voyage. That'll clear your head. A good night's sleep won't do you any harm either. I'm bedding down in this lifeboat. That one's yours. In you go – and, whatever you do, don't show your face until we're well out to sea.'

I didn't. I slipped under the tarpaulin and climbed into the rowing boat. It was dark and damp and terribly uncomfortable. I lay down in the bottom of the boat, shivering with cold, my eyes shut tight, wondering what would happen next. Was Dr Webster on my trail? Would Zapristi and I be caught and thrown into jail like my dad? Or would we drown at sea and be eaten by sharks? Or would I get to England after all and make my fortune? I squeezed my lucky dime and thought of Miss Taylor. Where was she now?

I don't remember it, but eventually I must have fallen asleep. The moment I woke up I realised we were out at sea. It wasn't just the swell of the water, or the sound of the waves hitting against the side of the ship; the air smelt quite different and the sun was beating down on the tarpaulin above me. It was morning.

I got to my knees and crawled to the edge of the lifeboat. I pushed up a corner of the sheeting and looked out. The sky was clear blue. There were seagulls floating overhead. At the far end of the deck I could see two sailors lashing a long rope around a mast. Standing watching them was a girl. She looked about eight. She had long curly hair and was wearing a blue checked dress. Suddenly, she turned away from the sailors and began cartwheeling across the deck towards the lifeboats. The moment she stopped she saw me.

'Hello,' she said. 'My name's Daisy. Who are you?'

Chapter Six

DAISY

'I said my name's Daisy,' repeated the girl. 'What's yours?' I didn't say anything. 'Don't you speak English?' said the girl, stepping closer to the lifeboat. 'You look English.'

'I'm American,' I said. 'From New York.'

'You've got a funny accent,' said the girl. 'I'm from London. Have you been there?'

'Isn't that where we're going?' I asked.

'Of course not, stupid!' said the girl, giggling. 'We left London weeks ago. We're going to Mexico!'

'Are the streets in Mexico paved with gold?'

The girl began to giggle again. 'I don't think so, but my papa says there's silver hidden in the hills. That's what we're going to find.'

'Silver?'

'Yes, lots and lots of silver. Papa says it's going to make us very rich. He's an explorer you see.'

'Yes, I see,' I said, but I didn't really.

'He's a lord too,' continued the girl, 'but he says being an explorer is much more important. What does your father do?'

'He's, he's a—' I hesitated. I didn't know what to say.

'He's a wonderful man,' said a voice I recognised at once. 'He's a wonderful man and we miss him very much, don't we Max?'

It was Miss Taylor! I could not believe my eyes, but there was no doubt about it. There she was, standing on the fore deck of the *S.S. Miranda*, alive and well and looking exactly as she always had.

'Miss Taylor! Miss Taylor!' I scrambled out from under the tarpaulin and jumped into her arms. I hugged her as hard as I could. Her eyes were full of tears.

I had found Miss Taylor again. I didn't know whether to laugh or cry.

'What are you doing here?' I asked

'I had to get another job,' she said. 'I'm Daisy's governess now.'

'Is Dad all right?' I asked, looking up into her face.

'I'm not sure, Max,' she answered, putting me down and pulling a handkerchief out of her sleeve. She wiped her eyes. 'Your father's still in prison. They haven't started the trial yet. I'm sure he's innocent, but it's going to be difficult to prove.'

'Unless Dr Webster confesses,' I said.

'What do you mean?'

'I know it was Dr Webster who took the money,' I said.

'How do you know, Max?'

'I heard him say it when I was hiding behind the drapes in the drawing room. He laughed at Dad.'

'He's a horrible man.'

'Why didn't you go to the police?' asked Daisy. She

I DIDN'T KNOW WHETHER TO LAUGH OR CRY...

was always asking questions.

'Because I'm still only seven and they wouldn't have believed me,' I said.

'Psst!' The noise came from the middle lifeboat. 'Aren't you going to introduce me to your friends?'

The unshaven face of The Great Zapristi appeared from under the tarpaulin.

'Who is it?' squealed Daisy.

Zapristi was scrambling out of his lifeboat, still clutching his shiny top hat but looking very much the worse for wear. He offered Daisy and Miss Taylor an elaborate if somewhat unsteady bow and said, 'Ladies, allow me to present myself. I am The Great Zapristi.'

'He's famous the world over,' I said quickly, and then began to tell the story of how I'd hidden in the chimney to escape from Dr Webster, how I'd run away and found myself in Zapristi's dressing room at the Adelphi Theatre, how I'd become Ali, the Boy Wonder, how the New York All Stars had come to an end and how we had decided to set sail for England to make our fortune.

'That's a quite extraordinary story,' said Daisy's father half an hour later when, in the captain's cabin, Miss Taylor had made me repeat it to him word for word. 'I don't approve of stowaways and, by rights, I should put you and Mr Zapristi here in a rowing boat and let you fend for yourselves.'

'Oh, Papa, please don't!' said Daisy.

'I won't,' said Lord Dunbar, with a smile, 'but only because it turns out Miss Taylor knows young Max – and because sometimes a long sea voyage can be a little dull and it might be good to have a magician on board to entertain us now and then.'

'Your Lordship,' said Zapristi in his grandest voice, sweeping his crumpled cloak around him. 'In return for your great kindness, my young assistant and I will entertain you and your crew with some of the greatest marvels ever seen on the high seas. We will begin tonight by sawing the Lady Daisy completely in half!'

Daisy squealed, her father laughed and Miss Taylor led us out of the captain's cabin towards the cook's galley to find us some breakfast.

*

That evening, a little before sundown, The Great Zapristi did indeed saw Daisy in half.

Her father, Miss Taylor and the crew watched as Zapristi invited Daisy to step forward and climb into the magic cabinet that we had balanced across two barrels in the middle of the fore deck. Once inside the box, Zapristi made Daisy put her head through a hole at the top of the box and her bare feet out through another hole at the bottom. He then asked the ship's carpenter to find a saw and bring it to him.

While the audience held its breath The Great Zapristi carefully sawed the box in half and then stood between the two halves as, at one end, Daisy blew a kiss to her father and, at the other, waggled her toes!

*

For a week the *S.S. Miranda* steamed steadily south. Every morning Lord Dunbar insisted that I go to Miss Taylor's cabin with Daisy and share her lessons. Every afternoon The Great Zapristi taught us new tricks. Every evening, exactly an hour before the sun went down, we would put on our show.

It was on the morning of our eighth day at sea that the storm broke and Daisy was thrown overboard.

Chapter Seven
'MAN OVERBOARD!'

The storm seemed to come from nowhere. One moment the sky was blue, next it was grey, then it went black. One moment the sea was calm and flat, the next it began to heave and surge and swell, then great waves roared up at us and the whole ship was tossed into the air.

I was standing on the quarterdeck with Daisy – we had been practising cartwheels until it was time for our first lesson of the day – when a gigantic wave swept like a tornado across the ship. I clutched at the ship's rail as the whole vessel was flung into the air. As we crashed down into the sea again another gigantic wave swept over us. Daisy had disappeared.

One of the sailors must have seen her being thrown into the fierce black waves. 'Man overboard!' he yelled. 'Man overboard!'

As the ship sank and rose and the water crashed down on to us, Lord Dunbar staggered across the deck, shouting, 'Man the lifeboats! Save my daughter! For God's sake, save my daughter!'

The sailors could barely stand as the ship rocked to and fro, and up and down, and the wind howled in our ears and the spray of the sea blinded our eyes. They tore the tarpaulin off the first of the three rowing boats – the one where I had spent my first night on board the *S.S. Miranda* – and tried to ease the boat over the edge of the ship's rail and into the water. Just as the rowing boat touched the water another gigantic wave swept the ship up towards the blackened sky. As we crashed down again, the rowing boat was smashed into pieces. It was then I saw Daisy, clinging to a piece of the wreckage.

Through the shrieking of the storm I heard her voice. 'I'm coming!' I called. Grabbing a lifebelt and holding it high above my head I clambered on to the ship's rail and leapt out into the dark water.

I landed right by Daisy. Her face was blue, her lips were black. 'I can't hold on any longer,' she sobbed. I was only about a yard away from her in the icy water, but it took all my strength and what seemed like forever to swim that yard. When I reached her, she let go of the piece of wood she had been clinging to and flung her arms around my neck.

'You've saved her!' shouted Lord Dunbar from one of the lifeboats. 'Thank God, you've saved her!' He was standing at the front of the boat with a rope in his hand. Behind him were two sailors rowing with might and main. As the lifeboat reached us, Daisy's father threw the rope towards us. I grabbed it and tried to tie it under Daisy's arms. 'Hold the rope!' I shouted into her ear. 'Have you got it?' I never heard her answer because suddenly we were swept thirty feet into the air on the crest of a terrifying wave.

That was the last I saw of Daisy. I thought it was going to be the last of me too, but as I was tossed up and down in the tempestuous water another rowing boat came out of the darkness towards me. There was a man alone in it struggling to keep hold of the oars. It was Zapristi.

'Here!' I yelled. 'Over here!' I don't know if he heard me, but the rowing boat lunged towards me and I grabbed hold of the oar. Zapristi gripped my arm and heaved me into his boat.

For what seemed like hours we rode the waves. The wind howled and distant lightning flashed and cracked in the blue-black sky. Ice-cold rain and sharp salt spray beat down on us as we clung to the sides of our little boat and rocketed up and down, up and down, higher and higher, and lower and lower, on a terrifying, uncontrollable, never-ending roller-coaster ride.

And then, suddenly, it stopped. As mysteriously as the storm had come, it disappeared. The dark clouds vanished, the sea became quite still. I lifted my head and looked up at a brightening sky. I turned around and peered out across the flat ocean. Whichever way I looked I could see as far as the horizon. The storm had gone. And the *S.S. Miranda* and Lord Dunbar and Daisy and Miss Taylor had gone too.

'We've lost them,' I whispered. And then I thought of my father, locked in prison, waiting for his trial. I looked at Zapristi, lying exhausted at the other end of the boat, his eyes half-closed. 'I've lost all my money too,' I said, sadly.

'Have you also lost your faith in The Great Zapristi?' He lifted his battered top hat and passed it to me. 'Look in there, young man.'

I looked inside the hat and there, tucked inside the lining, were my eight dollars – plus a one hundred dollar bill.

'Wow!'

'That's magic!' said Zapristi happily. 'Lord Dunbar gave me a similar bonus. He seems to have enjoyed our shows.'

'How come the money's in here?' I asked.

'A shoebox is not a safe place for large quantities of cash, my boy. It's too obvious. I always say, "If you've got something special to hide, keep it under your hat!'"

*

All day our rowing boat drifted in the Atlantic Ocean and then, just as night was beginning to fall, we sighted land. I was lying exhausted in the bottom of the boat when Zapristi suddenly got to his feet and began shouting and waving his arms in the air. 'Land ahoy!' he cried, 'Land ahoy!'

He was so excited that for a moment it seemed as if he would capsize the boat. 'Look, boy,' he said, 'dry land! We'll be there by sunset.'

We were. Zapristi took the oars and rowed hard and fast and in less than an hour we were dragging our lifeboat up on to a sandy beach.

'I'm never going on a boat again, that's for sure!' said Zapristi firmly.

'I wonder what happened to the others,' I said, looking out over the vast expanse of sea.

'Don't look back,' said Zapristi. 'Never look back! Only look ahead. Who knows what we will be doing an hour from now?'

'LAND AHOY!'

Believe it or not, an hour later I was washed, changed, and sitting at the ringside of the Barnum & Bailey Circus enjoying a new kind of food that was all the craze that year: a hot dog!

As we trudged up the beach, not knowing where we were or what was going to happen to us next, we saw ahead of us a gigantic candy-striped tent. 'I'd recognise that Big Top anywhere,' exclaimed Zapristi. 'That's the Barnum & Bailey Circus, the most famous circus in the world. This must be Florida.'

'How do you know?' I asked.

'Zapristi knows everything!' he said with a laugh. 'Do you remember I told you about my last assistant?'

'Pandora?'

'The Exotic Princess Pandora, if you don't mind. I told you she left me to join the circus. Well, this is the circus she joined.'

'I thought you said she was eaten by a lion?'

'Did I?' said Zapristi rather quickly. 'Are you sure?'

Chapter Eight

'YOU'RE IN THE CIRCUS NOW!'

Pandora hadn't been eaten by a lion. She might have been because she was the lion-tamer's assistant and, at every performance, she had to put her head inside the mouth of a huge African lion who had the sharpest (and yellowest) teeth you ever saw.

Finding Pandora was easy. All the circus performers' caravans were parked around the back of the Big Top. 'The lions' travelling cage will be right at the far side,' said Zapristi confidently. 'Lions have a very distinctive smell. You can't miss it.'

We followed our noses and found the lions. We found Pandora too. She was busy sweeping out the inside of the cage.

'Princess Pandora?' said Zapristi, bowing towards her.

She looked up and, for a moment, I thought she didn't recognise him. Then she moved to the edge of the cage and peered through the bars. 'Zapristi – is it really you? What's happened to your hat? Where's your silver-topped cane? What have you been up to this time?'

Pandora came out of the cage and took us into her caravan.

Zapristi told our story and, when he had finished, Pandora turned to me and asked, 'Is all this true?'

'Yes,' I nodded. 'It's all true.'

'What you two need is a hot bath—'

'Oh no,' interrupted Zapristi. 'I'm not going near water, hot or cold, ever again!'

Pandora laughed. 'How about a hot meal then, and a change of clothes?'

'That's more like it,' said Zapristi, smacking his lips.

'And then I'll introduce you to The Great Gonzago.'

'Who's he?' said Zapristi, suspiciously.

'He's our ringmaster. He's in charge. You'll like him. Everybody does.'

*

When we met The Great Gonzago later that night – after we had changed into the clothes that Pandora had found for us, feasted ourselves on hot dogs and watched the circus, cheering specially loudly when Pandora put her head inside the lion's mouth – I liked him a lot.

Everything about Gonzago was big. He wore big black shiny boots and a big black shiny top hat that was twice the size of The Great Zapristi's. Inside his ringmaster's red frock coat he had a big tummy that wobbled like a giant jelly as he moved. He had big round eyes, a big broad grin and a big booming voice that filled the whole of the Big Top as he introduced the acts. Best of all, he had a great big heart and, as soon as Pandora had introduced us, he said, 'Boys, welcome to Barnum & Bailey's Circus! The Princess has told me all about you. Your worries are over. You're in the circus now!'

And we were. Within one week The Great Zapristi had become a star attraction, sawing Princess Pandora in half inside the lion's cage! I was transformed from being Ali, the Boy Wonder, into 'Mighty Max, the Pocket Ringmaster'. Pandora made me a ringmaster's uniform and my job was always to be at Gonzago's side and to copy everything he did. When he cracked his whip, I cracked mine. When he threw a big bucket of water over the clowns, I ran after them with a little bucket. When, in the grand finale, he rode around the ring on the back of a huge elephant, I followed right behind on the back of a baby one.

As the weeks rolled by, and our circus caravans rolled on from Florida up to Georgia and across to Alabama and Mississippi and Louisiana, we became firm friends. The Great Gonzago told me all about life in the circus and I told him all about my father

'Welcome to Barnum & Bailey's Circus!'

and Miss Taylor and Dr Webster and the missing million.

*

One day, it was when the circus had just arrived in New Orleans, he came into Pandora's caravan and said, 'Max, I've had a great idea! How much am I paying you?'

'Two dollars a week.'

'And how much do you need to get your dad out of jail?'

'Almost a million.'

'Right. So, at the rate you're going, it's going to take you ten thousand years to raise the money.'

'I know,' I said sadly.

'Cheer up,' said Gonzago, slapping his fat tummy, 'and read this.' He held out a newspaper for me and Pandora to see.

'What's it about?' asked The Great Zapristi who was lying on his bunk snoozing under his shiny new top hat.

'It's about the Niagara Falls,' said Gonzago, 'and your once-in-a-lifetime chance to cross them on a tightrope at the most dangerous point – and make your fortune!'

'You can count me out,' said Zapristi pushing his hat back over his eyes. 'I'm not going anywhere near water again – ever!'

Pandora read out the newspaper article:

THE CHALLENGE OF THE CENTURY!

The Niagara Falls, on the border between the United States and Canada, where Lake Erie overflows into Lake Ontario at the rate of 10,000 gallons per second, has long been regarded as one of the wonders of the natural world and North America's greatest tourist attraction. Now the editor of the Niagara Falls Gazette has issued an amazing challenge. On behalf of the hoteliers of Niagara he is offering a reward of $10,000 to anyone brave enough to risk life and limb by crossing the world famous Falls on a tightrope.

'How much did you say?'

Gonzago laughed.

'Yes, Max, she said ten thousand dollars!'

'For ten thousand dollars,' I said, 'I'll do it!'

'How old are you, boy?' asked Gonzago.

'I'm nearly eight,' I said.

'That means you're seven, Max,' said Gonzago, firmly. 'And if you cross the Niagara Falls on a tightrope at the age of seven, young Max, I reckon you'll make a lot more than ten thousand dollars.'

Chapter Nine
WALKING THE TIGHTROPE

'Can you walk a tightrope, Max?' asked Pandora.

'I don't know,' I said. 'I've never tried.'

'I'll teach you,' said Zapristi from under his hat. 'It's as easy as falling off a log.'

'The circus arrives in Niagara in sixteen weeks' time,' said The Great Gonzago. 'That's the beginning of July. We'll start drumming up publicity right away. You won't be Mighty Max, the Pocket Ringmaster, from now on. You're about to become "Maximilian Rich, the Boy who walks the Tightrope"!'

The Great Zapristi was right. Walking the tightrope was easy. At least, it was easy when the rope was just three feet off the ground and tied between two caravans. It wasn't too bad either ten feet up and tied between two trees. To my astonishment, even thirty feet in the air and stretched right across the Big Top of the Barnum & Bailey Circus I could do it without difficulty. So long as you let your feet guide you and you never look down, you won't have a problem.

Walking a tightrope is like riding a bicycle. It's a knack. Once you can do it, you can do it. The world's most famous tightrope walker was a Frenchman called Monsieur Blondin. He was only five when he started, much younger than me, and throughout his long life he travelled the world, walking the tightrope. He never fell off. He was still balancing on the high wire when he was over seventy. He went everywhere: Australia, New Zealand, India, Europe, America. He was the first person to cross the Niagara Falls on a rope, back in 1859, but Blondin made his crossing near the suspension bridge where the waters are calm. I was to cross between Terrapin

Point and Table Rock, where the Falls are at their fiercest and most dangerous.

As, week by week, the circus travelled north across the country, my skill on the tightrope increased and The Great Gonzago encouraged me to be ever more daring. Seven weeks before we reached Niagara the rope was stretched above the lions' enclosure.

'Ladies and gentlemen,' roared the ringmaster. 'Tonight, for the very first time in the history of this or any other circus, the amazing Maximilian Rich, the boy who walks the tightrope, the infant wonder of the age, the most daring seven-year-old on earth, will, before your very eyes, attempt his most difficult – his most outrageous – his most dangerous feat. He will cross a tightrope suspended above an open-topped cage filled with man-eating African lions!'

The audience gasped as Pandora let the lions run into the cage and I stepped on to the high wire. Since I didn't look down I couldn't see what there was to be frightened of – but my heart pounded louder and faster all the same.

I was becoming quite famous. Articles about me

THE AMAZING MAXIMILIAN RICH

appeared in the newspapers. Photographers came to take pictures of me on the tightrope above the lions' cage. The Great Gonzago was in a state of high excitement.

'I've never known anything like it,' he laughed, his mighty tummy wobbling up and down with delight. 'Everyone wants to see the boy who walks the tightrope! It's standing room only at the circus all week and at the Falls they reckon at least fifteen thousand people are going to show up to watch you – and you're going to get an extra dollar a head for each of them! That's a fifteen thousand dollar bonus on top of the ten thousand dollars you're guaranteed. Max, you're going to be rich!'

'I need a million,' I said.

'I know,' said Gonzago, 'and you'll get it. This is just the beginning. When you've conquered the Niagara Falls, we'll have you crossing the Grand Canyon!'

'But what if I don't cross the Niagara Falls?' I gulped.

The Great Gonzago stopped laughing. 'How do

you mean, boy?'

'What if I fall off?'

'Don't say that,' said Pandora.

'Don't be ridiculous,' said Zapristi. 'Remember who taught you to walk the tightrope!'

*

The week before we set off for Niagara Falls the circus was in Buffalo, in New York State. On Saturday afternoon, between the shows, I was sitting in Pandora's caravan counting out my money. I had three hatfuls now, so much, in fact, that I kept it all in a strong metal box.

I had just reached $1,000 when there was a sharp knock on the caravan door. I didn't answer. I could tell at once who it was. I could smell him. As I slammed shut the lid of the box, the door slowly opened and Dr Webster came in. Softly, he closed the door behind him and touched his hat by way of greeting.

'Congratulations, Maximilian. I hear you're quite a star these days.'

'What do you want?'

'I want to have a little talk, that's all. It's taken me quite a while to find you.'

'You tricked my dad into signing those papers, didn't you?'

'Tut-tut, Maximilian. Who told you that?'

'You did! I heard you admit it! You stole the money.'

'So you *were* hiding behind those drapes. I thought as much. In fact, that's what I wanted to talk to you about.'

Dr Webster walked towards me. 'Come now, Maximilian, we need to talk.' As hard as I could, I flung the strong metal box at him. He caught it with ease and laughed his horrible laugh. 'What's this? A little present for your father's old partner?'

He was leaning up against the wall at the far end of the caravan now. There was a sneer on his face. 'Yes,' he hissed, 'I swindled your father, but no one has heard me admit it – except for you. And now I've found you, young Maximilian, you are going to promise me never to breathe a word of what you heard to another living soul. Do you understand, boy? If you utter one word of what you know, your life won't be worth a five cent candle!'

'Help!' I yelled. 'Help! Police!'

'Shut up, boy!' Webster dropped the metal box and lunged towards me – but he didn't get very far because, as he tried to grab me, a dagger flew sharply past my head and pinned his coat against the wall; then another came and trapped his hat; then another and another and another.

I looked up and there was Zapristi, grinning from ear to ear, with three more daggers still to throw. Off they went – whoosh-thud, whoosh-thud, whoosh-thud!

Dr Webster was well and truly trapped.

'Gotcha!' chuckled The Great Zapristi.

'Let me go!' yelped Dr Webster.

'Certainly not,' said Zapristi firmly. 'You'll remain our prisoner until the police arrive to cart you off to jail where you belong. I heard every word of your interesting confession and as I'm neither seven years old nor a son of the accused, the police, the judge and the jury will have no difficulty in believing me.'

Dr Webster squirmed against the wall.

'Stop wriggling, man,' said Zapristi, making a smacking noise with his lips. 'Stop wriggling or we'll have to let you cool your heels in the lions' cage. We've got three man-eaters, you know.'

'Yes,' I said happily. 'And it's just coming up to their dinner time.'

Chapter Ten
'NEVER LOOK BACK'

The lions didn't get Dr Webster, but the police did. They came and arrested him, and Zapristi told them everything he had heard.

'He's a bad man that Webster,' said Zapristi shaking his head.

'Smelly too,' said Pandora, pinching her nose.

'When do you think they'll let my dad out of jail?' I asked.

'As soon as they get Webster to New York.'

Zapristi sounded so confident. Pandora seemed

less sure. 'Won't they need to find the missing money first?'

'Max is going to make a million, anyway,' boomed Gonzago. 'I know it!'

*

We arrived at Niagara on Monday. My attempt to walk across the Falls wasn't due to take place until Sunday. The Great Gonzago had chosen the date with care – it was the Fourth of July, 1896. When the great day came, I didn't feel nervous. Oddly enough, I didn't feel anything.

At ten o'clock on the dot a horse-drawn carriage arrived at the Big Top and took me and Zapristi and Pandora and Gonzago on the three mile ride up to Terrapin Point. For the last half-mile we had to travel on foot and Zapristi and Gonzago carried me through the crowd on their shoulders. Everyone was cheering, but I couldn't hear the cheers because of the roar of the Falls. It was like the rumble of thunder and it never stopped.

The rope I had to cross was three and a half inches wide and 1,100 feet long. It was suspended a hundred and fifty feet above the roaring waterfall.

Through the mist and spray I could barely see the other side. Zapristi handed me the long pole I used to help me keep my balance. I stepped up to the edge of the Falls.

'Don't do it!' shouted Pandora.

'He'll be all right,' said Zapristi. 'I know my Max.'

'Don't do it,' pleaded Pandora.

I took the lucky silver dime from my pocket and tossed it one last time. 'Heads I go.' It was tails. 'I'm going anyway. I'm doing this for Dad.'

The Great Gonzago was standing on a soapbox addressing the crowds through a gigantic megaphone. 'Ladies and gentlemen, you have come today to witness the greatest wonder of the age – Maximilian Rich, the boy who walks the tightrope, will now cross the mighty Niagara Falls! Ten, nine, eight...'

'Remember,' said Zapristi, 'it's no different from the rope in the Big Top – a little longer, that's all.'

'...six, five, four...'

Pandora leant over and kissed me. 'Good luck!'

'...three, two, one...'

And out I stepped on to the rope. The crowd roared. I could hear Gonzago on his megaphone, 'And there he goes, the pride of the Barnum & Bailey Circus, stepping out into history...'

At first, I walked quite quickly, putting one foot lightly in front of the other, almost running along the rope. I tried not to listen to the cheering behind me. I didn't want to hear the roar of the water below. As I got further along the rope and the cheering became more distant and the roar of the Falls grew louder, I began to move more slowly. The wind seemed against me now and the spray from the Falls was soaking my feet and making them heavy. Step by careful step, one foot slowly in front of the other, I inched my way forward, head beating, heart pounding. And then I slipped! As well as soaking me, the spray from the Falls had made the rope wet and, as I put my left foot firmly in front of my right, it skidded forward, no more than an inch but it was enough for me to begin to lose my balance. The pole slipped from my hands and went tumbling down

THE POLE SLIPPED FROM MY HANDS...

into the Falls, far, far below.

Through the megaphone I heard a different voice. 'Steady, boy, steady.' It was Zapristi. 'Balance with your arms now.'

'I can't go on,' I thought. The crowd was silent, but the roar of the Falls thundered on. I began to turn my head back towards Terrapin Point. 'Don't look back!' yelled Zapristi. 'Never look back. Never look back!'

I looked straight ahead and put one foot firmly in front of the other. Through the spray of the Falls I could begin to see the crowds standing waiting for me at Table Rock. 'You're going to have to be brave, boy, brave and strong.' That was what my father had said. On I went. The crowds were cheering again. 'I'm doing this for you, Dad. I'm doing this for you. And for Miss Taylor.'

And, suddenly, through the mist and the spray, I could see them both, my father and Miss Taylor, standing side by side at the far end of the rope. Lord Dunbar and Daisy seemed to be with them.

'This is a dream,' I thought. 'Or have I died and

gone to heaven?'

But it wasn't a dream. I was alive and well and stepping off the tightrope and into my father's arms.

'Well done, boy,' he said, hugging me close. 'I am so proud of you. You were brave and strong.' I didn't tell my dad how frightened I had been. I just hugged him tight and knew that I was happier now than I had ever been.

The crowd roared and cheered and people threw their hats in the air as I rode on my father's shoulders.

For he's a jolly good fellow,
For he's a jolly good fellow,
For he's a jolly good fellow,
And so say all of us!

It wasn't until late that night that I heard the whole story: how Miss Taylor and Daisy and Lord Dunbar had survived the storm; how, because I had saved Daisy, Lord Dunbar had decided to try to rescue my father from prison; how they had arrived in New York just three days ago to find that Dr Webster had been arrested and most of the missing money had been recovered; how my father was freed; how they had heard about my attempt to cross the Niagara Falls on a tightrope and had rushed to stop me, but had arrived too late.

'You're a national hero, young man,' said Lord Dunbar shaking me by the hand.

'And I'm rich!' I said showing off my strong box bulging with dollar bills.

'What do you want to do with all your money?' asked my father.

'Can't you guess, Dad?' I said.

'Build a theatre?' he said, with a smile.

'Yes,' I said. 'Yes, let's build Rich's Playhouse – the most beautiful, the biggest and the best theatre in the world!'

'Will you be looking for a partner?' asked Lord Dunbar.

'Yes, please.'

'And you'll need someone to stage your shows, I imagine?' said Gonzago.

'Of course.'

'And you'll need stars!' said The Great Zapristi.

'Most certainly!'

'And a boy who walks the tightrope?' asked Pandora.

'Only during the holidays,' said my father firmly. 'Isn't that right Miss Taylor?'

'Is Miss Taylor going to be my governess again?' I asked.

'That wouldn't be very fair on Daisy now, would it?' said my father.

'Couldn't we share her?' I asked.

'Daisy's going to go to school in future,' said Lord Dunbar. 'Besides, I understand Miss Taylor doesn't plan to be a governess any more.'

'I am hoping to be married, Max.'

My mouth went dry. I had only just found her again and I was going to lose her almost at once.

'If it's all right with you,' she said very softly, 'I am going to marry your father.'

'Yes,' I said, grinning from ear to ear, 'it's all right with me,' and I cartwheeled across the room.

GYLES BRANDRETH is an author and broadcaster and worked in the theatre, television and publishing before becoming the Member of Parliament for the City of Chester in 1992 and joining the government as a Junior Whip in 1995. Although his mother is based in California, his brother in North Carolina, and his great-great-grandfather was a New York Senator (at about the time Max was having his first adventures), Gyles Brandreth lives in England with his cat, Felix, his three children, Benet, Saethryd and Aphra, and his wife, Michèle Brown, with whom he founded the award-winning Teddy Bear Museum in Stratford-upon-Avon.

MARK EDWARDS was born in Surrey and brought up in Kent, where he studied Fine Art at Medway College of Art. In 1974 his life changed completely when he moved to the extreme Northwest of Scotland, where he now lives in a remote cottage with his wife and three children. Mark has illustrated covers for many adult books but is currently concentrating more on children's books – often using his own children as models.

SIMON AND THE WITCH
by Margaret Stuart Barry

Simon's friend, the witch, is loud and outrageous and has a mean-looking cat called George. She behaves atrociously and can't help showing off, but she has a book of spells and a magic wand – and she's the best friend Simon has ever had.

THE MILLIONAIRE WITCH
by Margaret Stuart Barry

The witch has lost her pension book so there's no money for her and no food for George, her long-suffering cat. Simon suggests she gets a job and she tries lots of different things – even singing outside the Town Hall with her friend the Tramp. Then Granny Grim dies and leaves the witch something in her will. Something that will make her a millionaire!

SIMON AND THE WITCH
IN SCHOOL
by Margaret Stuart Barry

When the witch discovers she has lost her magic touch, Simon has the answer: "You'll just have to come to school and learn to read." But, once in the classroom, the witch is too busy causing chaos to learn much.

£2.99

THE
ENCHANTED HORSE
by Magdalen Nabb

The magical story of Irina, a little girl who finds a dusty wooden horse in a junk shop. Irina's mother and father have little time for her, even though it is Christmas, so Irina spends all her time loving and caring for the little horse made of wood – until one night, the horse stamps its hooves and whisks Irina away on an enchanted gallop through the night. This is the first of many secret rides, but when the enchanted horse hears the hooves of the wild horses, she gallops away from Irina who fears she'll never see her beloved horse again. But the horse does come back, and leaves Irina a very special present.

Children's Choice for the Smarties Award

KING HENRY VIII'S SHOES
by Karen Wallace

When Catherine finds a beautiful golden box in the maze at Hampton Court, little does she realise that it contains a shoe belonging to none other than King Henry VIII of England! And she is even more surprised when that larger-than-life monarch from Tudor times comes back – to twentieth-century England – to find his shoe. Catherine and her class mates learn all about Henry VIII and he finds out that in the twentieth century, kings can go shopping, go to burger bars and even ride on a bus!

£2.99

SPIDER McDREW
by Alan Durant

Spider McDrew is a hopeless case.
Everybody says so. He's so busy
dreaming he's often one step behind
everyone else. But he does have a
special talent for surprises. Whether
playing football or performing in
the school play, Spider *always* has a
surprise in store.

DISASTER WITH THE FIEND

by Sheila Lavelle

"Sabotage!" said Angela, "That's how we'll fix the cookery contest! We'll put something really nasty in Delilah's cake!" As usual, Angela's plan means that Charlie gets into trouble, but this time nothing turns out quite as Angela intended.

HOLIDAY WITH THE FIEND

by Sheila Lavelle

Charlie would rather have gone on holiday with a killer whale than Angela Mitchell, even though she promises not to get Charlie into any trouble. Things get off to a bad start when Angela dyes Charlie's hair... with disastrous results!

£2.99

Order Form

To order books direct from the publishers, just make a list of the titles you want and send it with your name and address to:

Dept 6,
HarperCollins Publishers Ltd,
Westerhill Road,
Bishopbriggs,
Glasgow G64 2QT

Please enclose a cheque or postal order to the value of the cover price, plus:

UK and BFPO: Add £1 for the first book, and 25p per copy for each additional book ordered.

Overseas and Eire: Add £2.95 service charge. Books will be sent by surface mail, but quotes for airmail despatch will be given on request.

A 24-hour telephone ordering service is available to Visa and Access card holders on 0141-772 2281.